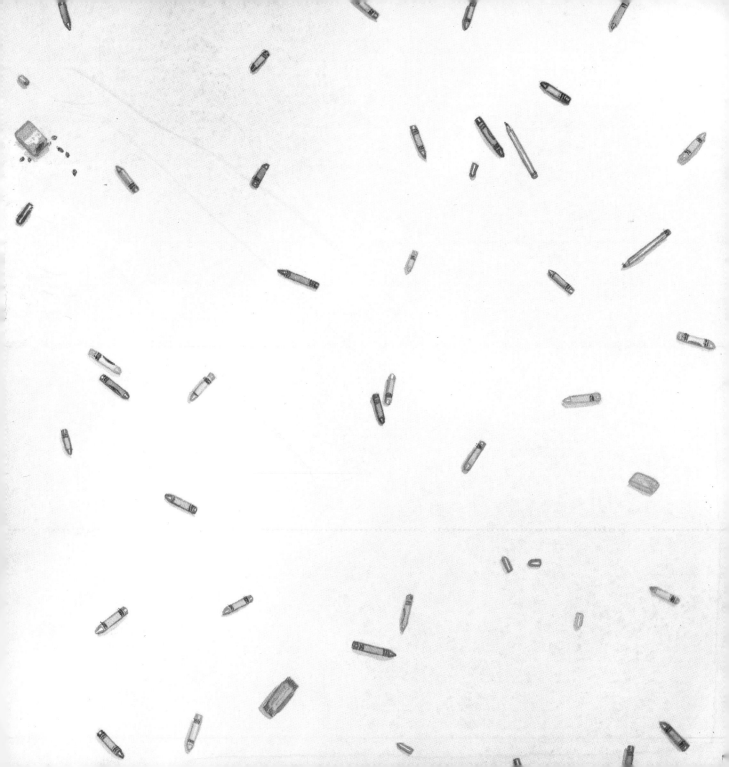

Time for School, Nathan!

by Lulu Delacre

SCHOLASTIC
HARDCOVER

SCHOLASTIC INC. / New York

For Mom, Arturo, and Ana-Mita,
who have always so relentlessly encouraged me.
Thank you.

A LUCAS • EVANS BOOK

Copyright © 1989 by Lulu Delacre
All rights reserved. Published by Scholastic Inc.
SCHOLASTIC HARDCOVER is a registered trademark of Scholastic Inc.

No part of this publication may be reproduced in whole or in part,
or stored in a retrieval system, or transmitted in any form or by any
means, electronic, mechanical, photocopying, recording, or
otherwise, without written permission of the publisher. For
information regarding permission, write to Scholastic Inc.,
730 Broadway, New York, NY 10003.

Library of Congress Cataloging-in-Publication Data
Delacre, Lulu.
Time for school, Nathan / by Lulu Delacre.   p.   cm.
Summary: Nathan the elephant triumphs on his first day of school
when he learns how to divide his attention between school and his
jealous best friend, Nicholas Alexander.
ISBN 0-590-41942-0

[1. Elephants—Fiction.   2. Schools—Fiction.   3. Friendship—Fiction.]   I. Title.
PZ7.D3696Ti   1989   [E]—dc19   88-38826   CIP   AC

12   11   10   9   8   7   6   5   4   3   2   1   9/8   0   1   2   3   4/9
Printed in the U.S.A.   38

First Scholastic printing, September 1989

R-r-r-r-r-r-r-r-i-i-i-i-i-n-g!!

It was seven o'clock
and time to get up.
"Wake up, sir!" cried Nathan's best friend,
Nicholas Alexander.
"Today is our first day of school.
Please hurry! We mustn't be late."

"Of all the things
we've done
and places
we've been together,"
continued Nicholas,
"school will be the best."

"No, no, no," Nathan
quickly replied.
"You don't understand.
I want to go
all by myself."

"All by himself
indeed," muttered
Nicholas.

After breakfast,
Nathan quickly
gathered his
school things…

and waved good-bye
to Nicholas.

Nathan jumped into the bus,
and off he went to school.

At school
the teacher asked the children
to sit in a circle for roll call.
"Now, please tell me your names
in a loud, clear voice," she said.
"Amy!"
"Chris!"
"Paul!" the children called out.
"Alicia!"
"Ritchie!"
"Nathan!"
"NICHOLAS ALEXANDER!" said a tiny voice.
Nicholas Alexander? thought Nathan.

"Will everyone please be very quiet,"
said the teacher as she opened
a large storybook and began to read.
Suddenly Nathan heard the familiar
little voice singing.
"Where are you?" whispered Nathan.
"You weren't supposed to come...."

"Nathan!" said the teacher.
"Please be quiet while I read."
"But…"
"And don't play with the coatrack!"

After the story, the children gathered into groups
for playtime.
Some children got felt boards, some got clay,
and others got toy cars.
Ritchie and Alicia were in Nathan's group.
They got a huge puzzle.

The three playmates
worked long and hard.
Just as Nathan very carefully
put in the last piece,
he felt something tickling him…
SPIKITY, SPIKITY,
SPIKITY, SPAK!
went the puzzle.

"Nathan!" cried Ritchie.
"You ruined our puzzle!
I'm not playing with you anymore."
"Neither am I!" exclaimed Alicia.

"I think this is all Nicholas' fault."
whispered Nathan.

At recess time, Nathan
was the last one to leave the room.
All the children followed the teacher,
trotting, jumping, running, and sliding.
But not Nathan.

Nathan just sat under a tree all alone.
After a while, Nicholas called out to him.
"Sir," he said, "what is the matter?"
"Nothing," said Nathan.

"Please tell me," said Nicholas.
"Well," said Nathan,
"it's just that...I thought
this was going to be a great day.
But everything turned out wrong,
and it's all your fault,
and I don't want to go to school
ever again!"

Nicholas scratched his chin
and thought hard. "Mmm...,"
he said. "I must admit I might
have played a *little* part in all this."
"Why?" asked Nathan.

"You see," replied Nicholas,
"if you go to school every day
and make friends, I won't be
your best friend anymore."
"Of course you will," said Nathan.
"You will always be my best friend."

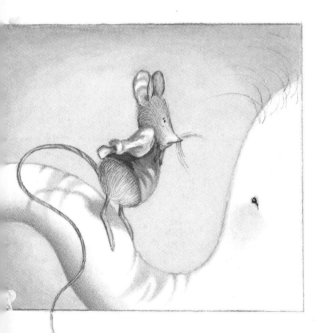

"Really?" said Nicholas.
"Really," said Nathan.
"I guess I was well…
jealous," said Nicholas.
"I'm sorry."

After recess, Nicholas promised to be good
for the rest of the day.
When Nathan told Alicia and Ritchie
he was sorry about the puzzle,
they said they had forgotten all about it.

So at snacktime Nathan traded his raisins
for Ritchie's peanuts.
Alicia gave Nathan her small chocolate bar.
Later, the teacher gave all the children paper and crayons.
"I have an idea!" cried Nathan, remembering
a trick Nicholas had once taught him.

Nathan folded the paper in three parts
and explained that they wouldn't know what
the picture would look like until the end.
First Alicia drew the head and
front legs of her favorite animal.
Then Ritchie drew the body of
his favorite animal.
Finally Nathan drew the back legs
and tail of his favorite animal.

When they finished,
they eagerly opened the paper.
"Wow! It's pretty neat!"
exclaimed Alicia.
"I didn't know this trick," said Ritchie.
"It sure is great!"
"My friend Nicholas showed me
this," said Nathan.

When the teacher saw the drawing
she taped it to the wall
for all the children to see.
"It is the very best picture," she said.
Alicia, Ritchie, and Nathan were so proud,
they all held hands and did a little dance.

Finally school was over.
Nathan grabbed his backpack
and started nibbling on his chocolate bar.
Nicholas walked with him to the bus.
"Oh, my!" said Nathan, "School *is* wonderful!
I think I've made two new friends."
"Two new friends in one day!" said Nicholas.
"That's quite an accomplishment, my dear sir.
And you did it all by yourself."

"Oh! Nicholas," said Nathan.

"I'm very happy in school, but I can't wait for *our* weekend treat."

"This Sunday I'll be going for a ride on a hot air balloon. Do you want to join me?" asked Nicholas.

"Yes! Yes! I'd love that!" cried Nathan.

"On Monday morning," said Nicholas, "you can tell your new friends all about it."

"You know something, Nicholas?"
"Tell me, sir."
"I'm glad we're best friends."
"Me, too, sir,"
said Nicholas with a smile.

"Me, too."

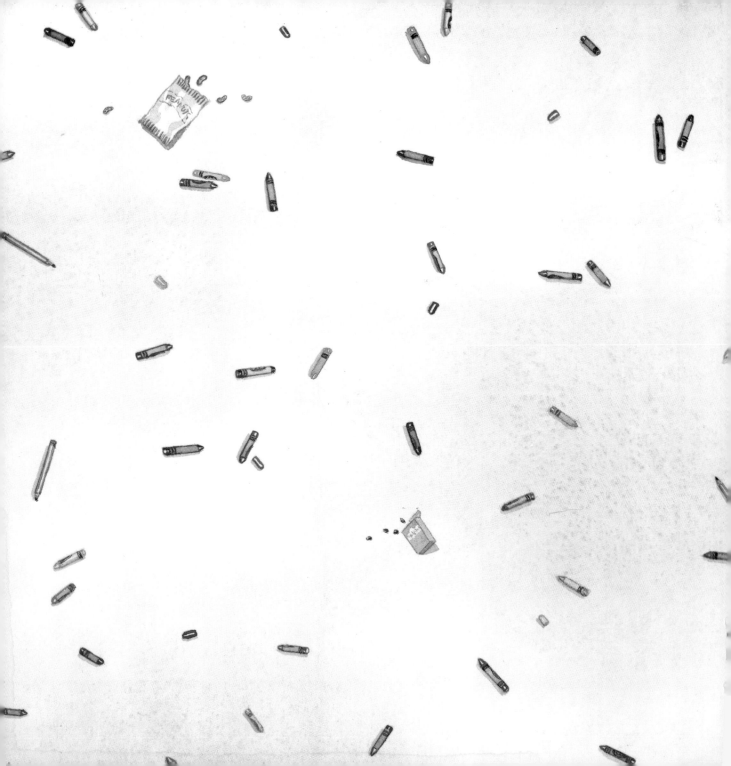